Musical Delights

John Mansfield Thomson

Musical Delights

A CAVALCADE OF CARTOON AND CARICATURE

THAMES AND HUDSON

Gerard Hoffnung

Printed and bound in Hungary

Page 1: A violinist at the Queen's Head Tavern, Newgate St, London. John Nixon, 1784

Page 2 and 3: Alfred Bendiner.

Prelude

What was it like to be present when Liszt or Paderewski performed? How strange did the avant-garde music of Wagner and Berlioz sound to the ears of a contemporary audience? What was the atmosphere of the eighteenth-century theatre? These and hundreds of similar questions arise as we listen to or read about music. The written word can tell us much, but the artist's pen or pencil, swiftly traversing the page, can capture the spirit of the moment in an incomparable way.

This collection of cartoons and caricatures distils the very essence of musical artists and events. Hogarth's ardent, roisterous singers are more likely to be true to the occasion than the studied portraits of a studio artist. Gillray, Rowlandson and Cruikshank move with the utmost ease from one level of society to another. Daumier opens a window on the homely musical pursuits and pretensions of the Parisian bourgeoisie and café artists. With the other brilliant caricaturists who surrounded Philipon and his journals, he illuminates the prodigious virtuosos of the period, and records the impact of the new music and instruments in a visual shorthand of the preoccupations and passions of the time.

Caricature is a continuing art. In our own century we have admired and enjoyed Beerbohm, Kapp, Searle and Hoffnung from Britain, Cocteau and Sempé from France, Kühne and Leitner from Germany, Bendiner from America. Each has a characteristic touch and vision.

'A good caricature, like every work of art, is more true to life than reality itself', wrote Caracci, the Italian artist who brought the art to public notice. His words may serve as the motto of this book.

J.M. Thomson
Wellington
January 1984

'Well actually, Miss Tonks, my Soul *is* in torment.' (Searle)

Practice Makes Perfect...

Ophicleide class at the Paris Conservatoire. Course for minors: prodigy section. The ophicleide is a large brass instrument made obsolete by the tuba, though Bernard Shaw held that it was born obsolete.

Cello class. (Forest)

The 'musical doctor' takes 'his scholars' through their scales.
(Rowlandson)

'The morsel one is obliged to swallow after dinner'. (Daumier)

A martyr to music. (Kühne)

'Ruddy music lessons . . !' (Searle)

Domestic Harmony

HARMONY before MATRIMONY.

The cats frolic while the lovers enchant each other, a volume of Ovid's love poems open on the table behind them. Cupid, in the wall plaque, is releasing his arrows.

MATRIMONIAL·HARMONICS.

All is changed. Cupid has given up and fallen asleep. The wife assails
her husband from the keyboard, while nurse, baby, cat and dog, not to
mention the hissing urn, add to the cacophony. (Gillray)

'A most fearful instrument. . . . The vulgarity of the cornet is
incurable', thought Bernard Shaw – players suffer at a Parisian
bourgeois dance. (Daumier)

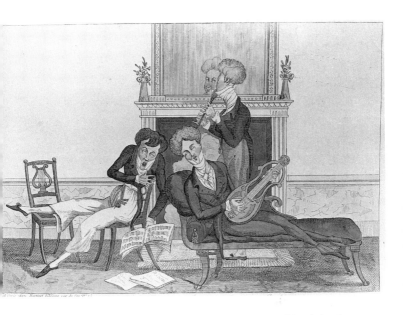

A narcissistic player of the chalumeau (the predecessor of the clarinet)
and two exquisite singers (with lyre) entertain themselves.

The hazards of sight-reading. (Cruikshank)

Glassmakers welcomed Adolphe Sax's new trumpet. ('Cham')

Gillray's merciless ridicule put an end to Lady Buckinghamshire's Pic-Nic Society. It was based on the French idea of ladies and gentlemen giving an entertainment to which they would bring their own food and drink.

The PIC-NIC ORCHESTRA

'Echo of Harlem' – reliving the jazz era. (Sempé)

Bravissimo !

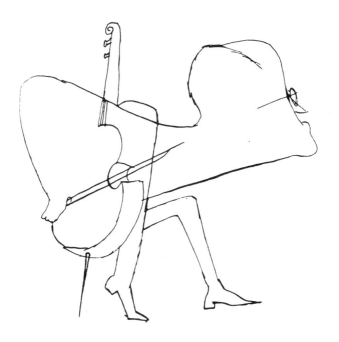

Mstislav Rostropovich, by Leitner

Silentium.

Introduzione.

Scherzo.

Adagio.

Adagio con sentimento.

Piano.

Smorzando.

Maéstoso.

Capriccioso.

Passagio chromatico.

Fuga del diavolo.

Forte vivace.

Fortissimo vivacissimo.

Finale furioso.

Bravo-bravissimo.

The virtuoso, by Busch

The soul of Paganini insinuates itself into the famous mid-nineteenth-century violinist Poussard. ('Cham')

Yehudi Menuhin, by Leitner

Franz Liszt on stage, captured by Jankó.

Liszt appears in his cassock. Haughty smile. Hurricane of applause.

First chords. Turns around to force the audience to pay attention.

Closes his eyes and appears to be playing only for himself.

Pianissimo. St Francis of Assisi converses with the birds. His face is radiant.

Hamlet's self-questioning. Faust's torment. The keys exhale sighs.

Reminiscences: Chopin, George Sand, beautiful youth, fragrances, moonbeams, love.

Dante: the Inferno; the damned and the piano tremble. Feverish agitation. The hurricane breaks down the gates of Hell. – Boom!

He has only played for us – while trifling with us. Applause, shouts and hurrahs!

A concert grand collapses under the weight of Liszt's charisma.

Artur Rubinstein, by Bendiner

Paderewski, the lion of the keyboard, caged for his own protection.

Gustave Doré, himself an enthusiastic gymnast, portrays the young
Offenbach's acrobatic antics while playing the cello.

Sargent, most fashionable portrait painter of the day, lulled those of his sitters interested, with recordings or live music. (Beerbohm)

The Divine Spark

Verdi, by Delfico

Verdi and Lulù

Erik Satie, by Cocteau

Francis Poulenc, by Cocteau

Caruso's impression of his friend Puccini in New York at a triumphant
rehearsal of *The Girl of the Golden West*.

Sergei Rachmaninov, by Bendiner

Thomas Arne, the composer of *Rule, Britannia*

Igor Stravinsky, by Leitner

Vaughan Williams, by Kapp

'The Unbelievable Glory of the Human Voice'

'Prima donna, primo tenore, basso profondo'. Doré comments on the
exertions necessary to earn vast fees.

'The world shall bow to the Assyrian throne!' Hogarth's depiction of the boisterous rehearsal for de Fesch's oratorio *Judith*.

'Now let's have your top E again, madam.' (Kühne)

The colourful coloratura soprano Mrs Billington (1765–1818) sings 'a
bravura air' from Arne's opera *Mandane*. (Gillray)

'Leader of a café concert, singing from 7 until midnight, with or
without trills, according to the taste of the customers'. (Daumier)

A musical party: in the background the composer Tosti (the tiny figure
at the piano smoking a cigar) and the famous singers of the day
Sammarco, de Reszke and Scotti. (Beerbohm)

Chalon's comment on Pierre Ignace Begrez's impassioned rendering of
Beethoven's *Adelaide*.

Kirsten Flagstad (1895–1962), one of the great Wagnerian sopranos of her day. Her Isolde has been described as 'a stately Nordic princess, more proud than passionate'. (Bendiner)

Self-caricature rarely has the same cutting edge: Caruso as the
swaggering Duke of Mantua in *Rigoletto*.

The gaunt, mop-haired figure of Berlioz – irresistible to nineteenth-century cartoonists. (Doré)

Gentlemen of the Orchestra

Provincial philharmonic society's method of reaching agreement.

Adolphe Sax's new instrument soon found its way into brass bands – it is played here with gusto. (Bouchot)

Bashful instruments section of the band of the National Guard. (Bouchot)

'Choir and orchestra'. John Hamilton Mortimer satirizes national types – English, Swiss, Italian and German.

Steam power helps the members of Grandville's surrealistic orchestra.

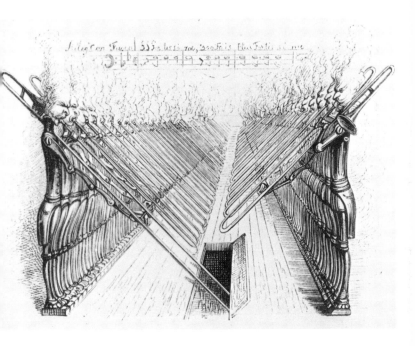

Grandville's 'Melody for 200 trombones', to be played 'with fire, *fortissimo*, repeated 300 times, then louder still'.

Drawing by J. Gilroy

GUINNESS for STRENGTH

G.E.1248.C

Maestro !

Sir Malcolm Sargent, by Leitner

Sir Thomas Beecham, by Kapp

Leopold Stokowski, by Bendiner

Pierre Monteux, by Bendiner

Renowned for his brisk tempi, Sir Michael Costa (1808–84) is shown by 'Spy' of *Vanity Fair*, with the baton tied to his wrist.

Toscanini in Paris,
by Caruso.

Rafael Kubelik, by Leitner

An Appreciative Audience

'Scene at Munich after an hour of compulsory Wagner'. (Daumier)

COMEDY in the COUNTRY.

TRAGEDY in LONDON.

Pub. May 29 1807 by Tho.º Tegg Nº 111 Cheapside

Rowlandson Sculp

70   Even the orchestral players respond to laughter and tears.
(Rowlandson)

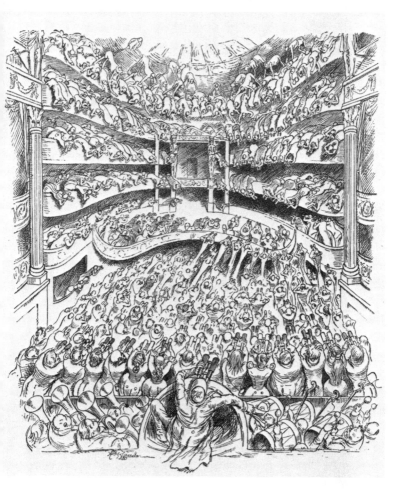

Wagner is a more diverting spectacle than that on stage. (Oberländer)

Hogarth's 'pleased audience at a play'. The severe-looking gentleman (beside the orange girl) may be a critic – they usually sat in the pit.

Coda

The Artists

Notes on the Artists and Illustrations

Numbers in brackets refer to the pages on which illustrations occur

Edward ARDIZZONE (1900–79). Famous illustrator of picture books and official war artist, he drew several coloured covers for *Punch* in the fifties. His designs for such firms as Guinness and Lyons were well known. [80]

Max BEERBOHM (1872–1956). English satirist, caricaturist and drama critic, succeeding Shaw as critic on the *Saturday Review* in 1898. His caricatures include the collections *The Poet's Corner* (1904) and *Rossetti and his Circle* (1922). [38, 52]

Alfred BENDINER (1899–1964). Cartoonist for the *Philadelphia Evening Bulletin*, he drew headings for special events for the daily Amusements Page before and during World War II. He was an accomplished artist as well as an architect: his work hangs in the Uffizi, the National Gallery of Art in Washington and the Philadelphia Museum of Art. He also served on university expeditions to Iraq and Guatemala, and wrote extensively. Frequent exhibitions are held of his work. [2, 3, 34, 43, 54, 65, 66]

Frédéric BOUCHOT (born 1798; died during the Second Empire). He drew for *La Caricature*, *Le Charivari* and *Le Petit Journal pour rire*; collaborated on albums with Daumier and Morin. [58]

Wilhelm BUSCH (1832–1908). Busch worked for various Munich journals such as *Fliegende Blätter* and *Münchener Bilderbogen*, where he developed the idea of the picture story, forerunner of the modern comic strip. His pictures hang in Zurich, Munich and Hanover. Probably the best known and best loved of German humorists, he withdrew to his native village after the rise of Imperialist Germany. [28–9]

Enrico CARUSO (1873–1921). The world-famous tenor was also renowned for his drawings. He became permanent caricaturist for an Italian newspaper in New York, *La Follia*. When offered $50,000 by Pulitzer for a monthly cartoon, he declined, admitting that *La Follia* paid him nothing. [42, 55, 68a]

Alfred Edward CHALON (1780–1860). Born in Geneva, he studied and worked in London, publishing illustrations for the works of Sir Walter Scott, and exhibiting at the Royal Academy. He was court painter to Queen Victoria. [53]

'CHAM', pseudonym of Amédée de Noé (1818–79). 'Cham' joined the team of artists on *Le Charivari* in 1843 and stayed there until his death, winning a reputation as a prolific and popular caricaturist. He was also author of several plays and a frequent visitor to England. No. 23 shows one of the seven varieties of saxhorns made by Adolphe Sax (1814–94), so much admired by Queen Victoria and used in British brass bands to this day. [23, 30]

Jean COCTEAU (1889–1963). One of the most eminent and versatile French intellectuals of the century, he excelled as poet, novelist, dramatist, critic, film director and artist. He collaborated with many of the celebrated artists and musicians of the time, and wrote a manifesto, *Le Coq et l'arlequin* (1918), that provided inspiration and a set of aesthetic principles for a group of young composers (including Poulenc) associated with Erik Satie called 'Les Six'.

George CRUIKSHANK, snr (1792–1878). The successor to Rowlandson, Cruikshank found himself in the midst of the triumphs and miseries of the Industrial Revolution. Renowned for his illustrations to Dickens, he drew over 10,000 caricatures and book illustrations in a long lifetime of eighty-six years. His wit and sense of humour are less mordant than Gillray's, partaking more of fantasy and kindness to human foibles. No. 21 is an 1822 French version of Cruikshank's *Humming Birds* (1819). [21, 22]

Honoré DAUMIER (1808–79). After the demise of *La Caricature*, Charles Philipon founded in December 1832 the daily paper *Le Charivari* ('a medley of sounds', 'a hubbub'). He attracted remarkable talents including Daumier, Doré, 'Cham', Gavarni, Gill and Grandville, all dedicating themselves to his campaign of 'warfare every day upon the absurdities of every day'. Daumier was his finest artist. [12, 20, 51, 69]

Melchiorre DELFICO (1825–95). The Neapolitan caricaturist Delfico left many affectionate portrayals of Verdi, a close friend. He also compiled, but left incomplete, a handwritten biography of the composer with his own illustrations. [40a, 40b]

Gustave DORÉ (1832–83). A gifted, self-taught violinist, Doré was deeply attracted to music; he frequented the opera, concert hall and musical salon and was a friend of some of the greatest artists of the age, such as Adelina Patti. His strong social conscience found an outlet in his searing illustrations of homeless men and women sleeping in doorways and prisoners exercising in pitiable circles, which appeared in Jerrold's *London* (1872). He also illustrated Coleridge's *Ancient Mariner*, Dante's *Divine Comedy* and the Bible. No. 47 is from *Two Hundred Sketches Humorous and Grotesque* (1867). Nos 36–7 and 56 are from *Le Petit Journal pour rire* (1856). [36–7, 47, 56]

Eugène-Hippolyte FOREST (born Strasbourg 1808). A pupil of Camille Roqueplan, his paintings were exhibited frequently in Paris. He produced several albums of prints, including caricatures in the style of Henri Monnier. He last exhibited at the Salon in 1866. [10a, 10b]

James GILLRAY (1757–1815). Hogarth's somewhat frenetic successor. His caricatures became collectors' items almost from the moment of their first appearance. Gillray's targets were mainly politicians, public figures, the foibles of high society, but above all the monarchy, George III and his consort Charlotte, whom he continually portrayed as paragons of parsimony and avarice. He was described after his death as 'the caterpillar on the green leaf of reputation'. [16, 17, 24, 50]

John GILROY (born 1902). Helped to build Guinness's tradition of witty advertising from 1935, but became famous also for portraits, whose subjects included members of the royal family. [62]

GRANDVILLE, pseudonym of Jean-Ignace-Isidore Gérard (1803–47). Grandville contributed surrealistic and satirical drawings to *La Caricature* and *Le Charivari* from 1830 to 1835. Both his political caricatures and his illustrations to such books as La Fontaine's *Fables* are enlivened by witty anthropomorphic inspirations. [60, 61]

Gerard HOFFNUNG (1925–59). Hoffnung's genius, tragically cut short at the age of thirty-four, expressed itself in a handful of marvellous little books and the brilliant satirical Hoffnung extravaganzas at the Royal Festival Hall in London. The savage intent of many of his predecessors was completely alien to him. He was much more interested in exploring the visual idiosyncrasies of the various musical instruments and their players. The theme from the Presto of Beethoven's Seventh Symphony decorates no. 26. [4, 9, 15, 26]

William HOGARTH (1697–1764). Hogarth raised the caricature from an aristocratic diversion to a work of art. In his two notable sequences *The Rake's Progress* (1735) and *The Effects of Idleness and Industry* (1747), he revived the medieval tradition of instructive moral pictures; *Marriage à la Mode* (1745), a satire on mercenary marriage and the decadent tastes of the time, served a similar purpose. Hogarth's friendships with actors, writers and entrepreneurs, including Garrick and Fielding, and his love of the theatrical led to his earliest musical caricatures: *A chorus of singers* (1732) and *A pleas'd audience at a play* (1733). *A chorus of singers* represents a rehearsal for the oratorio *Judith* (first performed in 1733), words by William Huggins, music by Willem de Fesch. [48, 70]

Janos JANKÓ (1833–96). Hungarian genre painter.

Edmond Xavier KAPP (1890–1978). Kapp was still a Cambridge undergraduate when he gave his first exhibition of caricatures. His 1919 London show, introduced by Max Beerbohm, launched him on a remarkably successful career, although Kapp deprecated any description of himself as a caricaturist. Nevertheless, his drawings of such composers as Delius and Schoenberg, to say nothing of that of Vaughan Williams reproduced here, have achieved the status of icons. [46, 64]

Gerhard KÜHNE (born 1928). Freelance short-story writer and cartoonist for the past thirty years for various German newspapers and magazines. [7, 13, 49]

Bernhard LEITNER (born 1938). A well-known German artist, trained as an architect, whose work has appeared in such journals as *Die Zeit*, *Forum* and *Die Furche*. He has drawn many of the outstanding performers and composers of recent times. [27, 31, 45, 63, 68b]

John Hamilton MORTIMER (1740–79). Mortimer had a leading position amongst artists who preceded Rowlandson, whom he had greatly influenced as a young man. His prodigiously talented work covers a wide range, from conversation pieces, historical paintings and self-portraits to satire, imaginary *banditti* and monsters. The engraving 'A choral band' or 'Choir and orchestra' (1776) owes much to Hogarth. [59]

John NIXON (1760–1818). Drew many well-known musicians. Thomas Rowlandson engraved scenes 'after Nixon', e.g. the etching coloured by hand *A Mad Dog in a Coffee-House*. [1]

Adam Adolf OBERLÄNDER (1845–1923). Genre painter and graphic artist. Honorary member of the Munich Academy.

Thomas ROWLANDSON (1756–1827). Friend and contemporary of Gillray, he found society more attractive than politics and began to specialize in his *tableaux de modes*, or social satires, about 1780. The consummate draughtsmanship of *Vauxhall Gardens* (1784) was often pressed into the service of a rumbustious, even coarse sense of humour. [11, 72]

Ronald SEARLE (born 1920). Ronald Searle's invention of St Trinian's became one of the great fantasies of the century. 'St Trinian's was indeed, in the words of our Founder "one great big trigger-happy family"', wrote Cecil Day Lewis in his preface to the last of the series. 'Though St Trinian's lie in ruins, the St Trinian's spirit will rise from her ashes, like a vulture from the feast'. The vitality, exuberance and whimsicality of his musical caricatures are unique. [4, 12, 37]

François Sénechal SEMPÉ (born 1932). Sempé is a gifted French caricaturist who in 1979 won the Grand Prix National des Arts Graphiques. He sold his first drawing, that of a violinist, at the age of fourteen and caught the attention of a local editor. Sempé began his book *The Musicians* in 1974, labouring over each drawing in scores of versions. His view of musicians covers the entire spectrum. [8, 18, 19, 25]

'SPY', pseudonym of Sir Leslie Ward (1851–1922). He succeeded 'Ape' (Carlo Pellegrini), whose caricatures put *Vanity Fair* (founded in 1868) on the map. The work of 'Spy' inclined towards portraiture rather than caricature. [67]

Sieglinde assists Siegmund in his heroic deed.

Acknowledgments

I thank Ronald Corcoran of Schott's, who gave me my first opportunity to write about musical caricatures, Margot Leigh-Milner, perceptive and indispensable researcher, and all the many friends and colleagues who offered help and suggestions, especially John Casey and his staff at the photographic department of Victoria University of Wellington, Gerald and David Coke and Richard Abram.

With thanks also to Mrs Alfred Bendiner and the Bendiner Foundation (illustrations on pages 2–3, 34, 43, 54, 65, 66), Mrs Edmond Kapp and Angela Lindsay (46, 64) and Mrs Eva Reichmann (38, 52). The drawings by Gerhard Kühne (7, 13, 49) are reproduced by courtesy of the artist and Uta Henning, Ludwigsburg; 38, 40a and 40b by courtesy of the British Library; 52 by courtesy of the Trustees of the British Museum; 44 by courtesy of the National Portrait Gallery; 53 by permission of the Victoria and Albert Museum; 62 and 80 by courtesy of Guinness Brewing; 42, 55 and 68a by courtesy of Covent Garden, Royal Opera House Archives.

Ronald Searle's cartoons (6, 14 and 39) © Ronald Searle, reproduced from *Souls in Torment* (1953) and *Merry England* (1956); Gerard Hoffnung's caricatures (4, 9, 15 and 26) reprinted from *Companion to Music* (1957), *Musical Chairs* (1958) and *Acoustics* (1959) by permission of Souvenir Press, London, and Riverrun Press, New York; François Sempé's caricatures (8, 18, 19 and 25) reprinted by permission of Workman Publishing Co., New York (1980); *Caruso's Caricatures* (42) by Enrico Caruso, compiled by Michael Sisca, Dover Publications Inc., New York, used with permission of the publisher; Bernhard Leitner's caricatures (27, 31, 45, 63 and 68b) © Erhard Friedrich Verlag, Hanover, 1967.

'Guinness for Strength' (Ardizzone)